THE END.

"Ooo, it looks like you've got a bit of egg on your face!" chuckled the Golden Hen. "You didn't really think they were made of gold, did you?!"

"Not **everywhere**,"
said Jack,
with a wink.

"We don't need riches,
do we?" said Jack's mum,
patting him lovingly
on the head.

CRUNCH!
CRUNCH!
CRUNCH!

"Not when we've
got each other."

"Oh no, I'm NOT,"
said Jack.

Just then up popped the
Golden Hen. "I wonder what
happened to my golden
eggs?" said the Golden Hen.
"I've looked everywhere."

. . . BUM," said the giant, in pieces on the floor.

"We're safe!" cried Mum. "Oh, Jack, you're such a good little pea."

"Oh no, I'm not!" said Jack.

"Oh yes, you are!" said his mum.

"WHAT?!
Nobody's chopping
ME in half!" shrieked
the beanstalk.

And with that, it started
to run, bringing the
giant crashing towards
the ground.

"WI-FI . . . FO . . . FUM . . .
I . . . THINK . . . I'M . . .
GOING . . . TO . . .
BUMP . . .
MY . . .

But the giant was hot
on their heels.

"WI-FI . . . FO . . . FUM . . .
YOU . . . CAN'T . . . HIDE . . .
YOU . . . CAN'T . . . RUN!"

"Quick!" shouted Jack.
"We're almost there!
Let's chop the beanstalk
in half so that the
giant can't catch us!"
"Good idea!"
gasped Mum.

Jack and his mum dived through the clouds . . .

. . . and started to climb down the wobbly beanstalk.

"HELP!" cried Jack and his mum, as they scrambled out of the cupboard and headed for the door.

"STOP . . . I'M . . . GOING . . . TO . . . EAT . . . YOU!" shouted the giant.

And with that, the giant melon-bot
flung open the cupboard.

"MUST . . . HAVE . . . PEA!" it said.

"WI-FI . . . FO . . . FUM, I . . . SMELL . . . PEA, GONNA . . . EAT . . . ME . . . SOME! BE . . . IT . . . ALIVE, OR . . . BE . . . IT . . . DEAD, I'LL . . . GOBBLE . . . ITS . . . LEGS . . . AND . . . CRUNCH . . . ITS . . . HEAD!"

"Quick!" cried Jack. "Let's hide in this cupboard!"

The door creaked open.

"WI-FI . . . FO . . . FUM, I'M . . . GONNA . . . FIND . . . YOU . . . HERE . . . I . . . COME!"

"I am the Golden Pineapple—
I mean Golden Hen and I lay
golden eggs! Just ONE of my
golden eggs will make you
rich beyond your
wildest dreams!"

"ONE?" snorted Jack.

"What do you mean
'just one'?!"

Then all of a sudden,
the ground started to shake,
and Jack and his mum heard
a loud, robotic voice.

In no time at all, they were through the clouds and could see a huge castle far off in the distance.

When they got to the door it was open, so in they went . . .

. . . and there on the table was a golden hen!

But it was too late. "HELP!"
he cried as he began to fall.

Could this be the end for Jack?

"Don't panic!"
called a voice
from below.

"OI! STOP CALLING ME GOOD! I'M EVIL! Mwah ha ha ha . . .

. . . ahhhh!" The beanstalk was moving about and Jack was losing his grip. "Keep still, you nitwit beanstalk!" yelled Jack.

The beanstalk just pointed.

So **good** little Jack started to climb.

"Maybe that nitwit Mango WAS telling the truth after all."

A huge beanstalk had grown and was stretching high up into the sky.

"Where are my riches then, Bean-cumber?" demanded Jack.

But nothing happened.

"Why don't we put them on toast!" suggested Mum.

"NO!" spat Jack. "I'VE BEEN TRICKED! These beans aren't magic at all!" And with that, he flung them out of the window.

"WHERE THEY BELONG!"

But in the morning, when Jack woke up, he found something very strange outside.

"WHAT DO YOU THINK I AM?!
SOME KIND OF NITWIT?!"

"Easy, dude – these are magic beans!
They will bring you riches beyond
your wildest dreams!"

Hmmm . . . interesting,
thought Jack.

And he dashed home to
show his mum the new
beans. "Go on then,
BE MAGIC!"
he shouted at them.

So off Jack went to market to sell the cow.

On the way, he met a mysterious mango. "Hey, dude. Nice cow! How about you swap me your cow for these beans?"

"You want me to swap my cow for some beans?" said Jack.

"He what?!

I mean, yes. I am VERY poor.
Whatever will I do?"

"There is only one thing we CAN do,"
said Jack's mum.
"We'll have to sell Daisy."

Jack didn't have a penny to his name,
but he did have a good, kind heart."

It's showtime in the supermarket
and the veggies are proud to present . . .
Jack and the Beanstalk.

"Once upon a time," Tomato began,
"there was a pea called Jack. He lived in
a tiny house with his mum and their
beloved cow, Daisy.

SUPERTATO

presents JACK AND THE BEANSTALK

SUE HENDRA
PAUL LINNET

TICKETS

SIMON & SCHUSTER

London New York Sydney Toronto New Delhi

Save the Children

Save the Children exists to make a lasting, positive difference so that every child gets a fair chance of a future they deserve. Covid, the climate crisis and increasing conflict are putting children at extreme risk and we are finding new ways to support the children who need us the most.

In more than 100 countries around the world, from Afghanistan to Myanmar to the UK, we help children stay safe, healthy and learning. We are constantly working with children fleeing conflict to find them a safe space to live.

Between November 2022 and August 2023, Simon & Schuster (UK) Ltd will donate £1.29 from the sale of this book to Save the Children Fund, a registered charity in England and Wales (213890), Scotland (SC039570) and Isle of Man (199).

For Laura – the force is strong in this one.

MIX
Paper | Supporting responsible forestry
FSC® C023419

SIMON & SCHUSTER

First published in Great Britain in 2022 by Simon & Schuster UK Ltd · 1st Floor, 222 Gray's Inn Road, London, WC1X 8HB

Text and illustrations copyright © 2022 Sue Hendra and Paul Linnet

The right of Sue Hendra and Paul Linnet to be identified as the authors and illustrators of this work has been asserted by them in accordance with the Copyright, Designs and Patents Act, 1988

A CIP catalogue record for this book is available from the British Library upon request

978-1-3985-1163-7 (HB) · 978-1-3985-1165-1 (eBook) · 978-1-3985-1232-0 (eAudio) · Printed in Italy · 10 9 8 7 6 5 4 3 2 1